RACE TO KITTY HAWK

Edwina Raffa
and Annelle Rigsby

Illustrated by Wellington Ward

SILVER MOON PRESS
NEW YORK

First Silver Moon Press Edition 2003
Copyright © 2003 by Edwina Raffa and Annelle Rigsby
Illustrations copyright © 2003 by Wellington Ward
Edited by Hope L. Killcoyne

The publisher would like to thank
Louis L. Chmiel, Wright Scholar, for historical fact checking.
Mr. Chmiel is curator at the Wright Brothers Aeroplane Company
and Museum of Pioneer Aviation in Dayton, Ohio.

For information:
Silver Moon Press
New York, NY
(800) 874–3320

Library of Congress Cataloging-in-Publication Data

Rigsby, Annelle.
    Race to Kitty Hawk / Annelle Rigsby and Edwina Raffa.-- 1st Silver Moon Press ed.
    p. cm. -- (Adventures in America)
    Summary: After being adopted by a woman in Dayton, Ohio, in 1903, orphaned
twelve-year-old Tess Raney uncovers a plot to foil the Wright brothers' quest to be the first
in flight, and takes great risks to make sure the plot fails.
    ISBN 1-893110-33-8
    [1. Orphans--Fiction. 2. Flight--Fiction. 3. Airplanes--Fiction. 4. Wright, Wilbur,
1867-1912--Fiction. 5. Wright, Orville, 1871-1948--Fiction. 6. Mystery and detective
stories.] I. Raffa, Edwina. II. Title. III. Series.

PZ7.R4435Rac 2003   *3180161*
[Fic]--dc21
                                                            2003043443

10 9 8 7 6 5 4 3 2 1
Printed in the USA

In appreciation to Joe, Anne-Marie, and Alicia for their loving encouragement.

–Edwina

To Mike, Ember, and Tia for their love, support, and inspiration.

–Annelle

ONE

"**T**ESS RANEY, GET YOUR HEAD OUT OF that freezing wind and shut the window! You'll catch a cold for sure and your clothes are getting all sooty."

Twelve-year-old Tess stuck her tongue out at her sister, Ellen. Then with a sigh, she did as she was told and sat back down on the hard wooden bench of the train car. Tess was tired of Ellen's constant nagging. Since the death of their parents from influenza earlier that year, Ellen had taken her role of older sister a bit too seriously in Tess's opinion.

"I was watching that flock of geese," said Tess. She pulled her feet up under her long skirt to keep them warm. She tried to comb her curly brown hair with her fingers.

"Tess, you waste too much time daydreaming about flying," said Ellen, shaking a finger at her, just like Mama used to do. "Now brush yourself off before Miss Carsdale sees what a mess you are."

At that moment, Miss Carsdale, the chaperone for thirty children from The Children's Aid Society in

New York City, was making her way through the train car. She was an earnest woman in her forties who had dedicated her life to placing city orphans in new homes on farms and towns in the Midwest. Her face showed the strain of such a grave responsibility. She rarely smiled.

When she reached Tess and Ellen, her hand flew to her mouth and her eyes widened in a look of dismay.

"Tess, why are you so filthy? What have you been up to this time?"

The overworked woman pulled a lace handkerchief from her pocket. Wetting the corner with the tip of her tongue, Miss Carsdale began to rub Tess's cheeks. Tess scrunched up her face and twisted her head away.

"I'll take care of her, Miss Carsdale," volunteered Ellen.

"Well, I hope so," said Miss Carsdale impatiently. "We'll be eating lunch soon and Ellen, I need you to help the little ones get cleaned up."

"Yes, ma'am," said Ellen politely. "I'll start right away."

With her green eyes and blond hair, Ellen always looks like a princess. I don't know how she keeps so clean, thought Tess. *Ellen never seems to get into trouble like I do, either.*

She watched her obedient sister take a washcloth from their carpetbag and work her way down the aisle toward the wash bucket. After dipping the cloth in icy water, she made her way back and began wiping Tess's face.

"Stop it, Ellen!" cried Tess, her blue eyes flashing angrily. "You're not my mother. Why, you're only one year older than I am. Go help the babies!"

Ellen shook her head in disgust and started toward the front of the car. She smiled sweetly at the small children huddled by the stove. One by one, she took them in her lap and gently cleaned their hands.

Relieved to be left alone at last, Tess returned to staring out the window at the Ohio countryside. She had never seen so much open space.

If I lived on a farm, I could have all the room I need to fly kites.

She began her favorite daydream about going to the park on Sundays to fly kites with Papa. It was the only day Tess could spend with her father because the other six days he loaded ships at the docks. She pictured Papa running behind her, lifting the red and gold Chinese kite to catch the wind. She remembered the way the colors danced in the sunlight. Papa always praised her kite-flying ability. He never seemed to mind if she got a little dirty. He knew it made her heart sing to be outdoors running in the wind with her beautiful kite, the next best thing to flying herself. She missed him so much.

Her sister's voice interrupted Tess's daydream. "Wake up. Miss Carsdale says we're almost there."

"Let's warm ourselves by the stove before we get off," suggested Tess.

Ellen and Tess moved slowly, steadying themselves as the swaying train rounded a curve. When they reached the black pot-bellied stove, Tess spread her open palms over the top. The fire was barely flickering, so Tess opened the grated door and flung a piece of coal inside. Sparks flew everywhere. An ember landed on Tess's jacket and started to smolder. Quickly, Ellen yanked off her sister's jacket and threw it on the floor. She stomped out the small flame with her high-topped boots. Then she placed the singed garment back over Tess's shoulders.

"You've got to be more careful!" hissed Ellen.

More sisterly advice. All she does is worry about me.

But Tess knew why Ellen was concerned. Tess did have a way of getting into all kinds of trouble. She didn't mean to, but things just seemed to turn out that way. Once she accidentally used salt instead of sugar in a pie she helped Mama bake for the church bazaar. Another time, Tess caught her head between the iron bars in the fire escape of their tenement building. Papa had to be called away from the docks to saw the railing and free her. The list of her misdeeds and mistakes went on and on.

"I'm sorry, Ellen," apologized Tess. "I just wanted to warm up the car."

"Warm up the car?" whispered Ellen crossly. "We're lucky that you didn't set the whole train on fire!"

Tess turned away from her sister and pressed her face against the etched-glass window of the train door.

"I won't do it again," she promised.

Tess squinted through the window past the landing and into the next car. She saw waiters dressed in white, starched uniforms setting tables in the dining room.

"I wish we could eat in the dining room instead of our car," she said wistfully. "It would be grand to be served a hot meal on such fine china!"

"Don't even think about going in there," warned Ellen. "It's against the rules and besides . . ."

Tess was spared the rest of Ellen's lecture when the locomotive whistle blew, signaling the train's approach to a small town.

"Everyone stay seated," Miss Carsdale called out. "We'll eat here first before stretching our legs."

Ellen helped Miss Carsdale pass out crusty bread and cups of milk. The children finished their light meal and then Miss Carsdale led them from the train to play in a nearby field.

Several older boys left the group and wandered over to the station platform. Tess followed them. A traveling organ grinder was entertaining a small crowd. His little brown monkey, dressed in a red vest and matching hat, was dancing to music and begging for coins. The orphans stood mesmerized while the monkey went through his routine.

"Oh, he's so cute!" cried Tess, bending down to shake the monkey's hand. Suddenly the train's departure whistle pierced the air and the monkey jumped into Tess's arms. She hugged the frightened creature close and patted him. Then Tess reluctantly handed the little animal back to his owner.

"Thank you for holding Ringo," said the friendly man. "Loud noises, they scare him, but he's fine now."

Just then Miss Carsdale approached the group on the platform and called, "Line up, children. It's time to go."

While the orphans climbed aboard the train, Miss Carsdale spoke to the organ grinder.

"Will you be going to the next town?"

"Yes," he replied, "Ringo and I are traveling in that direction."

"Would you ride in our car and let Ringo entertain the orphans?" asked Miss Carsdale.

"I'd be happy to," said the generous organ grinder. "They look like they could use some cheering up."

Tess watched him put Ringo into his cage and

carry the monkey onto the orphan train. The man took a seat by the door and set his monkey beside him. Tess pulled Ellen into the seat directly across from them.

Once the train was on its way again, the organ grinder set up his music box in the aisle. He attached the monkey to a long leash. As soon as he started playing, Ringo began to perform his funny act.

An hour had passed when Miss Carsdale announced, "The show's over children. Let's all give Ringo and his kind owner a big round of applause."

The children clapped enthusiastically and called for more. Miss Carsdale, however, remained firm, and the children soon settled down on the wooden benches to rest. The organ grinder returned Ringo to his cage on the seat beside him. With a smile and nod to Tess and Ellen, the man pulled his hat over his eyes to take a nap. In a little while the entire car was quiet, except for the organ grinder's snoring.

Still too excited to rest, Tess looked over at Ringo, who was running back and forth inside his cage.

Ringo can't sleep either. The organ grinder's loud snoring must be frightening him. He doesn't like loud sounds. I think he'd calm down if I held him for a little bit.

Tess made sure Ellen was asleep. Then she carefully eased past her sister and knelt down in the aisle by the cage. Ringo started to chatter excitedly when he saw her.

"Shhh . . .," whispered Tess. "If you're a good little monkey, I'll take you out for a minute."

Quietly, Tess unfastened the latch and lifted Ringo from his cage, but the monkey continued to chatter.

"Let's go out to the landing," Tess murmured to the monkey. "You'll wake up the whole car with your jabbering."

Tess stepped out onto the platform that connected the cars. She held Ringo up to the window of the dining car so he could see the people.

Suddenly the door to the dining car opened and a gentleman stepped out onto the landing to light his cigar. At that very moment, Ringo sprang from Tess's arms and scampered inside!

TWO

A HOME IN DAYTON

TESS WATCHED HELPLESSLY AS THE MON-
key jumped from table to table. Some diners
screamed. Others laughed. Ringo bounded onto a
chocolate cake and then leaped onto a waiter's
chest, leaving tiny chocolate footprints on the crisp
white uniform. When Ringo paused to eat a lemon
pastry off the dessert cart, Tess reached out and
grabbed his tiny collar. She pulled the mischievous
little creature into her arms.

Just then, an enraged conductor stormed straight
towards her and Ringo. Tess realized she was in big
trouble. Frightened by all the noise, Ringo jumped
onto Tess's head and held on for dear life.

"What's going on?" demanded the supervisor, glar-
ing down at Tess. "How did that monkey get in here?"

"I'm sorry, sir, he just got away from me," explained
Tess.

Everyone stared at her while she peeled Ringo
off her head and tried to calm him. Tess felt her
cheeks turning as red as Ringo's vest.

The conductor marched Tess and Ringo back

into the orphans' car where they found the organ grinder frantically searching for his monkey. By now all the children were awake. The older boys watched gleefully to see what would happen to Tess.

"Return that monkey to his owner!" ordered the annoyed man. Tess did as she was told. Then he turned to meet Miss Carsdale who was moving purposefully toward them.

"You need to keep a tighter rein on this girl!" he advised loudly, proceeding to describe in great detail the chaos that Tess had caused.

"If there's any more trouble," he finished at last, "I won't hesitate to put your group out at the next station!"

Without another word, he stomped off toward the dining car, leaving Tess to face Miss Carsdale.

"I'm so sorry," said Tess meekly. "I never meant for this to happen. I was only trying to comfort Ringo. You see, Ringo is frightened by loud noises."

"Taking care of that monkey is not your job!" cried the chaperone. "Your job is to take care of yourself."

Miss Carsdale struggled to regain her composure. Once she was calm, she spoke again.

"Tess, you have done a very bad thing. Go sit down and think about mending your ways!"

The children snickered as Tess sat down in disgrace. Ellen just shook her head. Several minutes passed.

Maybe just this once Ellen won't lecture me.

But that was not to be the case.

"We'll never get adopted if you keep upsetting Miss Carsdale," warned Ellen. "I promised Mama that I'd keep us together, but you're not helping."

"I'm *trying* to help," Tess argued.

"Then try harder," said Ellen testily.

During the rest of the trip, Tess took Miss Carsdale and Ellen's advice to heart and stayed on her best behavior. Miss Carsdale began to notice Tess's efforts and even smiled at her occasionally. Ellen gave fewer lectures and stopped mothering her so much. By the time the train reached Dayton, Ohio, Tess felt that both Miss Carsdale and Ellen had forgiven her.

As she got off the train with the other orphans, Tess wondered if Dayton would be her new home. Tess knew any children not adopted that day would have to return to the orphan train. They would ride to the next town where they would go through the same painful experience all over again. Tess was tired of traveling. She dearly longed for a place of her own.

Miss Carsdale instructed the orphans to stay together as they moved through the noisy bustle of the station. Tess, however, soon lagged behind to investigate the jets of steam that shot out from the locomotive. Ellen ran back to get her.

"You're too curious, Tess," she scolded. "Let's go!"

When the sisters caught up with the rest of the group, they saw Miss Carsdale talking with two women. The poorly clad children waited in the cold, rubbing their arms to keep warm. Finally Miss Carsdale turned to the group and clapped her hands to get their attention.

"These nice ladies have a hot breakfast waiting for you at their church," she announced. "We will walk there right now. Ellen and Tess, go to the end of the line and don't let anyone wander off."

The sisters took their place in back and the band of orphans started their trek through the center of town. They passed a grocery store, a print shop, a bicycle shop, and a hardware store. Several shop-keepers were sweeping autumn leaves away from their entryways.

When Tess and Ellen passed an emporium, they stopped for a minute to gaze at the fancy Victorian hats displayed in the department store window.

"Look at the ostrich plumes on that purple hat!" exclaimed Tess.

"And what lovely beaded handbags," added Ellen.

Miss Carsdale's voice interrupted their window shopping, "Keep moving, girls!"

"That woman has eyes in the back of her head," whispered Tess, running to catch up with the group.

Soon they came to a gray, stone building with a tall steeple. A sign on the lawn read, *United Brethren Church: Bishop Milton Wright*. The children went inside the church and trooped downstairs into the fellowship hall.

The large room was filled with round tables set for breakfast. A lectern, a table, and several chairs stood on a wide stage at the front of the room. When everyone was seated, a bearded man stepped to the lectern and raised his hands for silence.

"Welcome to our church. I'm Bishop Wright. In a

few minutes, you'll be served breakfast. Then you'll have a chance to meet people from our community who are interested in adopting."

"Each of you has much to offer," the bishop continued. "Remember that God is always with you. Now, let us bow our heads and give Him thanks."

After the children feasted on scrambled eggs and sausages, the church ladies cleared away the dishes. Miss Carsdale began organizing the children on stage. She placed the older children in back and the younger ones in front. Bishop Wright opened the double doors of the hall. Prospective parents began to file in and sit down.

Miss Carsdale stepped behind the lectern and the crowd quieted down to listen.

"I'm Miss Carsdale, chaperone for The Children's Aid Society in New York City. I'll get things started by introducing the children. Then you'll have the opportunity to talk with them. Should you make a decision to adopt today, please fill out the necessary papers at the table to my left."

Miss Carsdale began calling the children's names. As their turn approached, Tess felt a huge knot in her stomach.

"Ellen and Tess Raney," announced Miss Carsdale.

Ellen pulled her through the line so everyone could see them clearly. Tess's heart pounded so hard she was sure the audience could hear it.

"Ellen Raney is thirteen and her sister, Tess, is twelve," said Miss Carsdale. "They would like to be adopted together. Ellen is respectful of her elders and good with children. Tess is . . ."

Tess held her breath as Miss Carsdale paused, searching for words to describe her.

Then smiling, Miss Carsdale finished, "Tess is a fine girl who is curious and has a lively imagination."

Relieved their turn was over, Tess and Ellen melted back into the line. Finally Miss Carsdale finished her list. The orphans clattered down the steps and awkwardly mingled with the crowd. Most people were drawn to the little ones and lined up at the table to sign the adoption papers.

Tess and Ellen stood with fixed smiles on their faces like wallflowers at a dance. An hour dragged by, but no one approached them. Tess noticed Ellen's eyes filling with tears, so she took her to a chair at an empty table. Ellen put her head down and began to weep quietly.

"Don't give up hope, Ellen," said Tess, giving her sister's hand a reassuring squeeze. "I'll figure something out. Papa always said 'God helps those who help themselves.'"

As Tess comforted her sister, she glanced around the room. She noticed a plump, matronly woman sweep into the hall. The lady carried a wicker basket over her arm. The face of a fluffy white cat peeked out.

"Stay here, Ellen, I've got an idea!" said Tess.

She walked straight to the lady with the basket.

"What a precious kitty!" declared Tess.

"Her name is Fluffy," replied the woman, pleased to meet another cat lover. "She goes everywhere with me. Would you like to hold her?"

"Oh, yes!" replied Tess, carefully removing the cat from the basket. "Fluffy is the perfect name for her."

"Speaking of names, I'm Miss Harriet Hamilton. I'm late getting here because of a problem at my boardinghouse. Let's go sit in that corner. While you pet Fluffy, you can tell me about yourself."

Tess followed Miss Harriet and the two sat down. The lady was a good listener. Tess described her adventures on the train, leaving out the most damaging details of her escapades. Then she told Miss Harriet about the death of her parents. Tess finished her story by saying, ". . . and now my sister Ellen and I are trying to find a new home together."

"I came here today looking for one child," said Miss Harriet, "but I would very much like to meet Ellen."

"Of course!" cried Tess. "I'll go get her."

After carefully placing Fluffy back in her basket, Tess brought Ellen over to Miss Harriet. The woman's big smile put Ellen at ease and soon the three were deep in conversation.

"Girls," Miss Harriet said, "I've lived in Dayton all my life and when my parents died, I inherited our family house. There's a lot of upkeep on it, so I take in boarders to help pay expenses. But boarders come and go and frankly, I get a little lonely at times."

"I've given serious thought to adopting for some time now," continued Miss Harriet. "If you come to live with me, you will attend school. I believe education is very important for young women. You'll also be expected to help with chores around the house. If you agree to these things, I think we'll get along just fine."

She wants us! We can stay right here and become a family.

Tess looked at Ellen who grinned back at her and nodded her approval.

"Miss Harriet," said Tess. "We accept your offer!"

THREE

The Mysterious Boarder

CARRYING FLUFFY IN HER BASKET, MISS Harriet showed Tess and Ellen the way to the boardinghouse. As they turned onto Hawthorn Street, Miss Harriet pointed out a narrow house with a Victorian-style porch.

"That's where Bishop Wright lives with his two sons, Wilbur and Orville, and his daughter, Katharine. You saw Bishop Wright this morning at the church," explained Miss Harriet. "The Wrights are a talented family. Katharine teaches high school history and Latin. Her brothers own a bicycle shop, and in their spare time, they are building a motor-powered flying machine."

"A flying machine?" asked Tess. Her eyes twinkled with excitement. "Do you think I could see it?"

"It's not here in Dayton," explained Miss Harriet. "Wilbur and Orville have taken the parts and assembled their machine at Kitty Hawk, North Carolina. They've named it the Wright Flyer and they're conducting experiments with it on the sand dunes there. But since you're obviously interested in flying, Tess,

I'm sure Bishop Wright would gladly tell you about his sons' hobby sometime."

By now they had reached a white picket fence. Miss Harriet paused at the gate and swung it open.

"This is my boardinghouse, your new home," she announced proudly.

The girls gaped at the two-story white structure with green shutters at each window. Compared to their old apartment building in New York City, this house was a mansion!

"Leave your bag here in the foyer and I'll show you around the first floor," said Miss Harriet, ushering the girls inside. Ellen put down the tattered carpetbag that held their few belongings and the girls began the tour.

Gesturing to the left, Miss Harriet explained, "The boarders usually come here to the parlor after dinner."

The girls glanced into a room filled with overstuffed furniture arranged around the fireplace. Tess noticed a man in a wing chair reading a newspaper with the headlines, *Local Men Test Flying Machine*. She also saw Fluffy had already found a warm spot to nap by the fire.

"Let's go on to the kitchen," Miss Harriet continued. "My cook, Emily, can heat you some chicken soup."

Miss Harriet turned to the right and led the girls through a dining room where a crystal chandelier sparkled above the oval table. Ellen followed at Miss Harriet's heels, but Tess slipped back into the parlor. She wanted to read the article about the flying machine.

Tess walked up behind the chair where the man sat deeply absorbed in reading the front-page article. She leaned over the man's shoulder to get a closer look and accidentally bumped him.

The tall man stood up and glared down at Tess. His brown eyes narrowed into slits.

"What are you doing?" demanded the man gruffly, whipping off his gold-rimmed glasses.

"I just, I . . . I . . .," stammered Tess. But before she could explain, the middle-aged man slid the newspaper inside his gray suit coat and stomped out of the room.

All I wanted to do was see the article about the Wright brothers. Why did he have to act so mean?

Just then she heard Ellen calling. Quickly she headed toward the kitchen, putting the upsetting incident from her mind.

After a late lunch, Miss Harriet showed Tess and Ellen the upstairs floor.

"This will be your room," said Miss Harriet, pointing to the first door on the right. "The room next to yours belongs to Miss Selena Van Borg, an actress at the Victoria Theater."

Pointing to the door directly across from theirs, Miss Harriet continued, "Mr. Wendell Oppenheimer lives here. He's the mathematics teacher at the same high school where Katharine Wright works. The next door down is the lavatory. Our newest boarder, a friendly man named Mr. Thaddeus Hardwell, occupies the last room on the left. He makes his living as a photographer."

Miss Harriet showed the girls their bedroom. The good-hearted landlady opened the window to rid the room of its musty smell. She took two extra blankets from the high bureau and began spreading them on the wrought-iron beds.

"You'll probably need these tonight," she said. "Fall evenings in Ohio can be chilly. What was the November weather like in New York City?"

Ellen immediately reached for an edge of the blanket and helped Miss Harriet.

Tess sat down in the rocking chair beside her bed. She listened as her sister talked about their crowded tenement building where the pipes leaked and the wind blew through the cracks in the walls.

When Ellen finished her story she asked, "Miss Harriet, is there anything else I can do?"

"Actually, Emily could use some help in the kitchen," said Miss Harriet. "I'll take you down the back stairs. It's the quickest way to get there."

"And I'll unpack our things," volunteered Tess from her chair.

As soon as they left, Tess opened a deep drawer in the bureau. She tossed in the contents of the carpetbag. Then she shoved the bag under Ellen's bed. Satisfied that her job was done, she wandered to the end of the hall and looked out the window.

Tess daydreamed for several minutes and then decided she'd better get back to the bedroom. As Tess passed the door of the photographer's room, she noticed that it was ajar. A book with a glider on the cover lay on a table by the door. Pushing the door open a little wider, Tess saw that no one was there. Like a magnet, her curiosity drew her inside. Tess picked up the book and flipped through it, immediately recognizing diagrams of various gliders. She had studied pictures like those in a book Papa had once borrowed.

Mr. Hardwell must be interested in flying, too. Maybe he'll let me borrow this sometime.

Just then Tess heard Ellen coming up the stairs. She closed the book and returned it to the table. She left the room and hurried to meet her sister.

The next day was Sunday. Miss Harriet took the girls to the United Brethren Church for the eleven o'clock service. Afterwards, the congregation stood on the church steps greeting one another. Miss Harriet introduced the girls to a number of her neighbors, including her good friend, Katharine Wright, a woman in her late twenties.

"Harriet, you and the girls must come for Sunday dinner," insisted Miss Wright. "It will give Father and me an opportunity to get acquainted with Tess and Ellen. Do say you'll join us."

Miss Harriet accepted the invitation and soon they were all seated at the Wrights' dining table. Bishop Wright said grace. Then Carrie, the servant girl, brought in a heavy platter filled with roast beef and vegetables. After a few minutes of adult talk, Miss Wright turned to Ellen.

"What do you enjoy doing, Ellen?"

"I love to read," replied Ellen. "My favorite author is Louisa May Alcott."

"She's one of my favorites, too," agreed Miss

Wright. "I've read all her books."

"And Tess, what are your interests?" asked Bishop Wright.

"Kites!" replied Tess enthusiastically. "I think it would be wonderful to soar up in the air like a kite. Maybe one day I'll be able to do that!"

"My sons, Wilbur and Orville, are also fascinated with flying," said Bishop Wright. "They built lots of kites when they were about your age. In fact, right now they are camping near Kitty Hawk and working on a flying machine."

"I've told the girls a little about your mechanically-inclined sons," said Miss Harriet. "Have you heard from them lately?"

"Wilbur writes that the flying experiments are going well," replied the bishop, "but the weather in the North Carolina Outer Banks has been cold and blustery. High winds and blowing sand are a real problem. In spite of the weather, though, I think Wilbur and Orville might be close to putting a motor-powered flying machine into the air. Of course, others are also competing to be the first to fly, but we have faith in Wilbur and Orville."

"I hope Wilbur and Orville will be the first ones. They've both worked so hard," said Miss Harriet.

Then turning to Katharine, she asked, "When do you expect them home?"

"By Christmas," answered Miss Wright, "but it all depends on the weather. To get home, my brothers must hire a boat from Kitty Hawk and travel 35 miles across Albemarle Sound to Elizabeth City, North

Carolina. Sometimes, especially during the winter, they're delayed by storms. Once they reach the mainland, they have a day-and-a-half train ride from Elizabeth City to Dayton.

Tess listened carefully to the conversation. The subject of flying intrigued her and she wanted to memorize every detail of the Wrights' experiences.

"I do hope they'll get back in time for the holidays," said Miss Wright wistfully. "It's so quiet around here without them."

"Well, some quiet must be nice after teaching all day," said Miss Harriet with a smile. "Speaking of school, I'm taking Ellen and Tess shopping for clothes tomorrow. On Tuesday, I'll enroll them."

"Would you like me to tutor the girls every afternoon to help them catch up with their lessons?" offered Miss Wright.

"How nice of you," said Miss Harriet. "I'm sure the girls would like that."

Ellen and Tess nodded their heads in agreement.

As the apple pie was being served, Miss Wright suggested, "Girls, let's start the lessons tomorrow at four o'clock."

When the meal was finished, Bishop Wright excused himself to go upstairs to his study. Miss Wright took her guests into the parlor.

"Oh, Tess, look at all these wonderful books!" cried Ellen, rushing over to the bookcase. "Here's one of fairy tales and here's one of poetry."

Tess went straight to the set of encyclopedias. She pulled out the "K" volume and sat at a table by the window. She opened the book to the section on kites. Ellen finally selected a book of short stories and joined her sister.

While Miss Wright and Miss Harriet visited over cups of tea, both sisters read avidly for the rest of the afternoon. All too soon, it was time to return to the boardinghouse.

Later that evening, the boarders sat around the fireplace in the parlor, talking and listening to music on the phonograph.

When Tess and Ellen entered the parlor, Miss Harriet began introductions. First she introduced the actress, Miss Van Borg, who was dressed in a flowing evening gown.

Next Miss Harriet introduced Mr. Oppenheimer, a short, balding man who was setting up a game of checkers on a small table between the wing chairs. Tess moved closer to examine the game pieces on the board.

"Why don't we play a game?" suggested the mathematics instructor. Tess took the other chair beside the table.

Just then a tall man wearing gold-rimmed spectacles entered the parlor. Miss Harriet motioned for him to join the group. He crossed the room and sat down on the sofa. When Tess looked up from the checkerboard, she stared into the same brown eyes of the stranger with the newspaper!

"This is Mr. Hardwell, the nice photographer I told you about," said Miss Harriet. "Mr. Hardwell, this is Ellen and Tess Raney. They've come to live with me."

He's Mr. Hardwell, the nice photographer? But he was mean yesterday, hiding his newspaper from me.

Tess heard her sister say, "We're pleased to make your acquaintance, Mr. Hardwell."

Mr. Hardwell greeted Ellen warmly, then gave a curt nod to Tess.

She crossed her fingers behind her back, hoping Mr. Hardwell would not mention the newspaper incident.

Suddenly Tess remembered the book in Mr. Hardwell's room.

"Mr. Hardwell, you're interested in flying, aren't you?"

"No, I'm not interested in flying at all," said Mr. Hardwell firmly. "I'm a photographer. I'm only concerned with taking pictures."

"But you have a book on gliders, don't you?" blurted Tess.

"You're mistaken, young lady," denied Mr. Hardwell strongly. "I have no such book."

Turning to the other boarders, he flashed a big grin. "My interest in flying is strictly limited to bird watching."

Everyone laughed but Tess.

That's not true! He claims he's not interested in flying, but I saw him studying the newspaper article about the Wright brothers and I found his book on gliders. Mr. Hardwell is lying, but why?

FOUR

THE EMPORIUM

L ATER THAT EVENING WHEN TESS WENT to bed, she snuggled under her thick blanket and thought about Mr. Hardwell's lie.

Why did he tell the others he had no interest in flying when he has a book on gliders? Is he hiding something?

For an hour, Tess restlessly tossed and turned. Unable to relax, she began her favorite daydream about flying kites with Papa. Tess thought about the unfinished kite she and Papa had been designing right before he died.

Maybe I can still build that kite. I'll need money for materials, though. Tomorrow I'll ask Miss Harriet about finding a part-time job.

With that decision made, Tess soon drifted off to sleep.

On Monday morning Miss Harriet opened the girls' bedroom door and announced, "Breakfast in fifteen minutes."

The boarders had already eaten in the dining room, so Emily invited Tess and Ellen into the cozy kitchen. Fluffy was curled up in her basket by the stove. Miss Harriet came into the room and began to pet Fluffy while she outlined plans for the day.

"As soon as your chores are done, we'll go to Owen's Emporium to buy school clothes," said Miss Harriet. "Then we'll come home for lunch and later in the afternoon you'll go to Miss Wright's for your tutorial."

After breakfast, Miss Harriet assigned Ellen to sweep the dining room floor. She gave Tess a feather duster to clean the parlor. In Tess's haste to finish her job, she knocked over a floor lamp near the fireplace.

Ellen came running when she heard the clunk of the long metal pole against the floor.

"Look what you've done!" cried Ellen. "There's a rip in the lampshade. Miss Harriet won't like that."

Tess thoughtfully studied the tear. Then she turned the lamp around until the tiny hole faced the wall.

"Now, no one will notice," said Tess with a satis-fied smile.

"Well, I hope you're right," said Ellen doubtfully. "You must do your chores carefully so Miss Harriet won't be sorry that she adopted us."

"Oh, Ellen, you worry too much. She chose us and . . ."

At that moment Miss Harriet came into the room to check on the girls' progress.

"We're finished with our chores, Miss Harriet," said Tess, moving away from the lamp. "Where should I put this duster and broom?"

Miss Harriet showed Tess a little closet under the

back staircase where the cleaning supplies were kept. While Tess was putting the things away, Miss Harriet sent Ellen upstairs to get their jackets.

Tess took the opportunity to ask Miss Harriet about getting a part-time job.

"I'd like to earn some spending money."

"Why?" asked Miss Harriet.

"I want to buy materials to build a kite like the one Papa and I were designing before he died. Do you think I could find someplace to work on Saturdays?"

Miss Harriet paused a moment to consider Tess's question. Then snapping her fingers she said, "I know! Last week, Mr. Owen at the Emporium told me that he's looking for someone to help in his millinery department during the Christmas season. You could talk to him while we're shopping this morning."

"Oh, thank you," said Tess excitedly.

Soon Miss Harriet and the girls were walking briskly to Owen's Emporium. When they entered the store, a man in a pinstriped suit came forward to greet them.

"Good morning, Miss Harriet," said the man pleasantly. "And who are these lovely young ladies?"

"Mr. Owen, this is Ellen and Tess Raney. They've come to live with me."

"I'm pleased to make your acquaintance," responded Mr. Owen with a welcoming smile.

Then turning to Miss Harriet, he asked, "How may I be of service?"

"I'm here to outfit these girls. They'll need every-thing from shoes to hats."

When Tess heard the word *hats*, she nudged Miss Harriet's arm.

"Oh yes," Miss Harriet said, "speaking of hats, is the part-time job in the millinery department still available? Tess is interested in applying."

"Why, yes," said Mr. Owen. "Mrs. Wheeler, the supervisor, could use an assistant on Saturdays. It's our busiest day."

Mr. Owen spoke directly to Tess. "If you work here, you must follow your supervisor's instructions. Do you think you could do that?"

"Yes, sir," said Tess. "I'll try hard to do exactly what Mrs. Wheeler tells me and I'll be very careful with the hats."

"Fine," said Mr. Owen. "Report to Mrs. Wheeler Saturday morning. Your hours will be nine in the morning until six in the evening. How does that sound?"

Tess looked up at Miss Harriet, hoping she would approve of the arrangement.

"That sounds just right," said Miss Harriet. "Tess is most eager to earn some of her own spending money and she's a good worker."

Tess saw Ellen roll her eyes after Miss Harriet spoke.

I can do a good job, even if Ellen doesn't think so. I'll prove I'm just as responsible as my sister.

Tess thanked Mr. Owen and promised him that she would be there early Saturday morning.

Mr. Owen escorted them to the ladies' department, where they began to select school clothing. Tess chose a long navy skirt and white blouse. Ellen bought a similar outfit in green. They selected several other dresses before moving on to the shoe department.

Ellen found some dove gray high-button shoes. Tess chose a pair with hand-tooled flowers on each toe. They were much nicer than the hand-me-down boots from The Children's Aid Society. The high-button shoes made Tess feel like a queen as they walked home to the boardinghouse.

In the afternoon Tess and Ellen went over to the Wrights' house for their first tutorial. Miss Wright met them at the door and took the girls into the parlor.

After they were seated Miss Wright said, "Before we begin the lessons, let me tell you a little about myself. As you know, I live here with my father, Bishop Wright, and with my brothers, Wilbur and Orville. My mother died when I was about your age, so I understand how difficult it is for you right now. I, too, had to grow up quickly."

"I managed our household while finishing high school," Miss Wright continued. "Fortunately, my father believes in education for women so I earned my degree at Oberlin College. Now I'm teaching high school, running the household, and overseeing the cycle shop when my brothers are at Kitty Hawk."

Tess, her mind never far from flying, asked, "Have you seen the Flyer at your brothers' shop?"

"Oh yes, I've seen it, but only in parts. It's too large to assemble it completely in the building."

"I wish I could meet your brothers and hear about their experiments," sighed Tess.

"I'll be sure to introduce you when they come home," offered Miss Wright.

Tess's face beamed with delight. It was exactly what she had hoped Miss Wright would say.

"Now, let's get started. Tell me what you've been studying," said Miss Wright.

The teacher listened as Ellen bubbled over with details of her favorite subjects, literature and history.

"I think I've found a kindred spirit," Miss Wright said with a smile.

Next it was Tess's turn to share. She told Miss Wright that she liked math and science.

"I'll check around the house a little later," said Miss Wright. "I'm sure Orville has some science books you'd enjoy, but right now, it's time to begin your lessons."

Miss Wright gave them a grammar exercise and the girls started their assignment. When they finished, Miss Wright sent them home for their evening meal.

On Tuesday morning, Miss Harriet walked the girls to school. Tess was nervous. She dreaded being the new girl in class. She knew Ellen was nervous too because she barely said a word the whole way.

Tess began to feel more comfortable when she was chosen captain for a team at recess. After school, she waited on the steps until Ellen came out. They chatted about their day as they made their way to the Wrights' house for their tutorial. The rest of the week flew by.

On Saturday morning, Tess dressed in her new navy skirt and white blouse. Then she walked to Owen's Emporium.

A petite middle-aged woman was waiting for her in the hat department.

"Are you Mrs. Wheeler?" asked Tess politely.

"Yes, I am. You must be Tess Raney, my new assistant."

Mrs. Wheeler showed Tess the worktable covered with stacks of hats. Drawers mounted on the wall were filled with ribbons, feathers, and artificial flowers.

"After finishing the hats, I will put them here for you to wrap," explained Mrs. Wheeler. "Then take the packages to the back of the store for the errand boy to deliver."

Tess fell easily into the routine of working in the millinery department. She liked the busy store with shoppers crowding the aisles looking for Christmas gifts.

The next Saturday, Tess and Mrs. Wheeler worked hard from morning until night. It was dark outside when they finally finished.

As Tess walked home, her shoes crunched through piles of autumn leaves. Rounding the corner of Hawthorn Street, she noticed all the lights were off at the Wrights' house.

The Wrights must have gone out for the evening. Maybe they're seeing that new play at the Victoria Theater.

Suddenly, she saw a man dressed in black crawl out of the second-story window onto the ledge. He shut the window behind him and began crawling down the rose trellis!

FIVE

The Telephone Call

QUICKLY TESS HID BEHIND A WIDE OAK tree. She waited for a minute, then peeked around the trunk. The man was now on the ground staring in her direction. She pulled back behind the tree, her heart pounding like a bass drum. When she summoned the courage to look again, the mysterious figure was gone.

Tess ran as fast as her legs could carry her to the safety of the boardinghouse. She raced into the parlor and found Miss Harriet sewing by the fire.

"What's happened?" gasped Miss Harriet.

Tess sat down on the couch next to Miss Harriet and told her about the stranger on the rose trellis.

"He must have been a robber," concluded Tess. "What should we do?"

"I'll call the police this very minute," declared Miss Harriet.

Tess watched the landlady cross the room to the telephone mounted on the foyer wall. Miss Harriet lifted the receiver and cranked the handle to get an operator.

"Dayton police, please."

She spoke briefly into the mouthpiece and then listened for a minute before hanging up.

"A policeman is being sent over to the Wrights' house to investigate," said Miss Harriet. "That's about all we can do for tonight. In the meantime, why don't you go into the kitchen and eat your supper? I had Emily save you a plate of beef stew."

"Thanks for helping me," said Tess as she headed for the kitchen. "I hope they find that man!"

When Tess and Ellen came down to breakfast Sunday morning Miss Harriet was telling the other boarders about the break-in.

Setting a platter of hotcakes on the table, she said, "Here's Tess now. Come tell everyone about the thief."

Tess sat down and told her story as she helped herself to some pancakes.

"Oh, Tess," said Miss Van Borg. "You must have been terrified!"

"I was, so I hid behind a tree. As soon as the thief was gone, I ran straight to Miss Harriet."

"Well," said Mr. Oppenheimer, "I'm glad you reported the robbery!"

Mr. Hardwell said nothing. He concentrated on buttering his pancakes, showing little interest in the conversation.

While Miss Harriet moved around the table serving hot tea, she warned, "We must be on the lookout for any suspicious characters."

The boarders voiced their agreement.

Finally Mr. Hardwell spoke up. "Did you happen to get a look at the man's face?"

"No, it was too dark to see," admitted Tess.

"That's a shame," muttered Mr. Hardwell, passing her the syrup.

Taking the pitcher from him, Tess noticed fresh, deep scratches in several places across the back of his hands. She quickly looked away and began pouring the syrup.

Later that day, Miss Wright came by the boarding-house for Sunday afternoon tea. The boarders had gathered in the parlor. They were eager to hear her latest news about the robber.

"When we got home," said Miss Wright, "a police-man was waiting on our porch. He had us carefully check each room of the house, but thankfully nothing was missing. In fact, the policeman said he could find no visible sign of a break-in."

"It just doesn't make sense that a burglar would sneak into a house and not take anything," observed Miss Harriet. "Tess, are you absolutely sure you saw a man climbing out the Wrights' upstairs window?"

Everyone looked questioningly at Tess. She felt her cheeks grow hot.

"Yes, I'm sure," said Tess in a soft voice.

"Well then," said Miss Harriet. "We must all be careful to lock our doors and windows from now on."

After tea, Miss Wright extended an invitation to the boarders.

"Father and I would like you to join us at Thanksgiving dinner on Thursday."

"Thank you, Katharine. I'm sure we'd all enjoy that," said Miss Harriet, accepting for the group.

Thanksgiving morning dawned crisp and clear. After the church service, the invited guests gathered in the dining room of the Wrights' home.

Following Bishop Wright's prayer of thanksgiving, Carrie brought in a golden brown turkey and set it in front of him. While he expertly carved the fowl, she placed steaming side dishes of mashed potatoes, green beans, and butternut squash on the table.

Throughout dinner, Mr. Hardwell entertained the diners with funny stories about taking baby pictures. Then he moved into the subject of flying and began asking questions about Wilbur and Orville.

"Are your boys close to getting the Flyer up in the air?"

"Well, they are certainly hoping for a successful flight soon," answered the bishop.

"Where did they find a motor for the Flyer?" asked Mr. Hardwell.

Tess was surprised at the photographer's questions. *Hadn't he denied having any interest in flying?*

"Wilbur and Orville built their own lightweight motor in the cycle shop with the help of their mechanic, Charlie Taylor," explained Bishop Wright. "They drew sketches of the motor on scratch paper and tacked them over the workbench. That way they all could easily refer to them."

Katharine leaned forward to add, "But my brothers didn't just work from sketches. They also referred to detailed records that they kept in notebooks. Air pressure tables from their wind tunnel experiments come to mind. They took those notebooks with them out to their camp."

Seeing that Carrie was waiting with the dessert tray, Katharine quickly finished, "To be on the safe side, however, Orville put copies of the notebooks upstairs in Father's study."

While pumpkin pie and coffee were being served, Mr. Hardwell suddenly volunteered to take a picture of the group.

"What a nice idea," said Miss Wright. "You may set up in the parlor."

While the others lingered over their dessert and coffee, Mr. Hardwell went back to the boarding-house to get his camera. The diners were deeply involved in a discussion about a new automobile they had seen around town. Tess was the only one to notice Mr. Hardwell return with his camera bag and creep up the stairs.

Why is Mr. Hardwell taking his camera bag upstairs? The parlor is on the first floor.

Ten minutes later, Tess saw Mr. Hardwell tiptoe down the stairs and slip into the parlor. Questions whirled like windstorms in her mind, but she couldn't come up with any answers to explain Mr. Hardwell's suspicious behavior.

Shortly, he called everyone to assemble for the photograph.

As the diners entered the room, Mr. Hardwell arranged them for the photograph. He directed the girls to stand on either side of the seated women.

Then Mr. Hardwell motioned Tess to move forward. "Young lady, put your flower-toed shoes on the green stripe in the rug."

Tess stood where she was told and the group all held their pose as Mr. Hardwell's head went under the camera drape. Flash! A puff of smoke filled the room. Tess mentally labeled the picture "Our First Thanksgiving in Dayton."

A week after Thanksgiving, Tess and Ellen were attending their tutorial with Miss Wright. Ellen was furiously scribbling down words in an essay about her orphan train experiences. Tess could tell by the way her sister clutched her pencil that Ellen was reliving those difficult days.

I hope Ellen's not writing about Ringo and the organ grinder or about my singed jacket. Some things are better left in the past.

Tess returned to drawing her diagram of the box kite. As soon as the design was perfect, she planned to buy the kite supplies.

"Miss Wright," said Tess, "I'm still having trouble with the dimensions of the frame."

Just as Miss Wright leaned over Tess's shoulder to get a closer look at her work, the front door to the Wrights' house opened. A man in his early thirties with blue-gray eyes and a brown mustache strode into the parlor. He put down a small satchel and stretched his arms out wide.

"Orville!" cried Miss Wright, hurrying over to give him a hug. "It's so good to see you, but what are you doing home? Why didn't you write me and let me know you were coming?"

Then peeking around Orville she asked, "Is Wilbur with you?"

Orville laughed at his sister's stream of questions.

"It's good to see you too, Katharine," said Orville. "No, Wilbur is not with me. He's still at the Kill Devil Hills camp. We're having trouble with the Flyer's propeller shafts, so I volunteered to come back to Dayton to make new ones."

Orville looked over Katharine's head and saw Tess and Ellen staring at him. "I see you have company," he observed.

"Oh, where are my manners?" Miss Wright said. "These girls are Miss Harriet's newly adopted daughters, Ellen and Tess Raney. Girls, this is my brother, Mr. Orville Wright."

"Oh, Mr. Wright," said Tess excitedly, "I've been waiting to meet you! Miss Wright told us everything about your flying machine."

"Everything?" he asked, a hint of mischief in his eyes. "I hope she told you how to keep it in the air."

Tess laughed. She liked him immediately.

"Oh, Orville," said Miss Wright, pretending to be stern, "stop teasing my students!"

"What are you drawing, Tess?" asked Mr. Wright, moving closer to study her diagram.

"It's my kite," explained Tess. "Papa was helping me, but he died before we could build it. Now, I'm trying to make it myself."

"She even took a part-time job at Owen's Emporium to pay for the materials," added Miss Wright proudly.

"But I'm having some trouble getting the correct dimensions," lamented Tess.

"Well, Tess, you've come to the 'wright' place," said Orville, laughing at his own pun. "If you'd like, I could help you build it."

"Thank you!" said Tess eagerly. "I'd like that."

"When you come for your next lesson," said Mr. Wright, "bring your plan and we can finish it together."

With a smile, Mr. Wright picked up his suitcase and headed upstairs.

The following afternoon, Tess squirmed impatiently at the table in the parlor. She was eager to finish her kite design with Mr. Wright. Ellen and Miss Wright were working together on a history lesson.

At last Mr. Wright came into the parlor and walked over to speak to his sister.

"Charlie Taylor and I have started working on the new propeller shafts in the shop. It'll take about a week to complete them so I'll be home for a few days."

"I'm glad to hear that," said Miss Wright.

Mr. Wright then turned to Tess and said, "I'm ready to help you now. Show me your kite plan."

Mr. Wright pulled up a chair next to Tess and studied the carefully drawn design.

"This looks good," he said, "but I see one problem. In order to stabilize your box kite you need to change your frame proportions."

Tess watched intently as Mr. Wright removed a pencil from his coat pocket and made a few bold strokes.

"Oh, I see," said Tess. "I need to add about five

more inches to each horizontal stick."

"Exactly!" replied Mr. Wright, watching Tess correct her design.

"Now I can go to the hardware store and buy my materials," said Tess.

"You can build your kite in the cycle shop," offered Mr. Wright. "Bring your materials to the shop tomorrow afternoon."

The next day, Tess watched the school clock slowly tick off the minutes. Finally school was over for the day. She grabbed her jacket and went directly to the hardware store.

As Tess stepped into the heated shop, an elderly clerk called to her from behind the long wooden counter. Tess walked over and handed him her list of supplies. He scanned it quickly.

"Making a kite, are you?" asked the man pleasantly as he began to gather the string, paper, glue, and sticks.

"Yes," said Tess earnestly, "and Mr. Orville Wright is going to help me."

"Well, you've got a good man as your assistant," chuckled the shopkeeper.

After the clerk put everything into a paper sack, Tess paid him with some of the money she'd earned. She carried her supplies back to the boardinghouse.

At four o'clock, Ellen and Tess went next door for their lessons. Tess was immediately excused to go work with Mr. Wright.

When Tess arrived at the Wright Cycle Company, Mr. Wright let her into the closed shop. Late afternoon shadows darkened the front part of the shop, but a bright light glowed in the back room.

"This is where Wilbur and I built our flying machine," explained Mr. Wright, showing her the workroom.

Clearing away some small pieces of metal from a workbench, he said, "Put your things up here, Tess."

As Tess unpacked her supplies, she noticed the sketches of the Flyer's motor tacked on the wall above the workbench.

While they measured sticks and cut paper for the kite, Mr. Wright told Tess how he and his brother had become interested in flying.

"When I was seven and Wilbur was eleven, my father brought home a toy helicopter. That little toy fascinated us boys and we played with it until the helicopter completely fell apart. Then we experimented building other toy helicopters."

After they finished measuring, Mr. Wright said, "Tess, go get the handsaw on the counter in the other room so you can cut the sticks. Be careful. It's sharp."

Tess made her way through the darkened shop until she found the counter. Suddenly a prickle ran down her spine. Tess glanced over at the front window of the store. A man was peering into the shop's interior!

A moment later, the man stepped away from the glass. She saw him walk down the street and pause under a street light to check his pocket watch. It was Mr. Hardwell!

Why was Mr. Hardwell looking in the window? It's

obvious that this shop is closed.

Snatching the handsaw, Tess hurried back to the lighted workshop. Briefly, she considered telling Mr. Wright about seeing Mr. Hardwell at the window.

Should I tell Mr. Wright what I just saw? No, I'd better wait. I need to understand what's behind Mr. Hardwell's strange behavior.

By six-thirty that evening, the box kite was ready for a trial run. Tess wanted to fly it right then, but she was resigned to waiting until the next day.

"If there's a wind tomorrow, we'll try it out," promised Mr. Wright.

As they walked back to Hawthorn Street, she remembered to thank him for all his help.

When Tess entered the foyer, she saw Mr. Hardwell hunched over the hallway telephone. He stood with his back to her and was speaking in a low voice.

This is my chance to find out what Mr. Hardwell's doing.

She eased behind the parlor curtains and strained to hear Mr. Hardwell's hushed tones.

"The boarders are in the dining room, so it's safe for us to talk," said Mr. Hardwell. "I searched the Wrights' house several nights ago—the Saturday before Thanksgiving—but I turned up empty-handed. Fortunately on Thanksgiving, Miss Wright unwittingly revealed the exact location of the notebooks. I stole the notebooks and they're on their way to you in Pittsburgh.

"J. R.," he continued, "I've studied them. The notebooks are a gold mine of information! Those brothers have developed a new type of control system. They've designed curved wings with flexible tips which help control the direction of flight. There's much more, but you'll see it all when you get the notebooks. At any rate, our mechanics should be able to copy their designs."

Mr. Hardwell whispered with an unmistakable gloat, "Listen, partner, with our team working round the clock and our huge budget, we'll beat those Wright brothers at their own game."

Tess strained to hear Mr. Hardwell's voice as he lowered it one more notch.

"I went to their cycle shop today," he said, "but Orville Wright is using the place while he's in town. According to my landlady, he's leaving soon for Kitty Hawk. The day Wright leaves, I'll go to his shop and . . ."

Suddenly Mr. Hardwell hung up. Looking down, Tess realized that the flowered toes of her high-button shoes were showing beneath the curtain. She cautiously inched her feet back and held her breath. She was sure Mr. Hardwell would rip away the curtain at any moment. Seconds dragged by. Finally Tess bravely stepped out from her hiding place. Mr. Hardwell was nowhere in sight.

Tess ran straight to her room to think.

Mr. Hardwell is stealing from the Wrights, but I still have no real proof. It's his word against mine. What should I do?

SIX

TESS WAS WORRIED. SHE WANTED TO TELL someone about Mr. Hardwell's telephone call. She thought about telling Miss Harriet, but the landlady liked the photographer. Without real proof, the Wrights and the police wouldn't believe her either. They had found no sign of a break-in at the Wrights' house to verify her story.

I'll talk to Ellen. She's my sister so she'll have to listen to me.

Tess waited in her bedroom until Ellen came upstairs.

"We missed you at supper, Tess. Are you all right?"

"I've got a problem, Ellen, and I don't know what to do."

She sat down on Ellen's bed and took a deep breath.

"It's about Mr. Hardwell. He's not a photographer," stated Tess firmly. "He's a thief!"

"Oh, Tess, that's ridiculous. Your imagination has gotten the better of you!"

"No!" insisted Tess. "I'm telling you the truth. Listen to me!"

Tess listed all her suspicions about Mr. Hardwell—the newspaper incident, the lie about the glider book, the scratches on his hands, his sneaking upstairs on Thanksgiving, and his peering into the bicycle shop window. She ended her story repeating Mr. Hardwell's telephone conversation.

"He's working with a partner in competition with the Wrights and stealing their ideas," Tess concluded.

"Oh, Tess," sighed Ellen. "You've probably misunderstood Mr. Hardwell's actions and telephone call. But if Mr. Hardwell is involved in some scheme, you had better stay out of it."

"You don't understand, Ellen. Mr. Hardwell is stealing from our friends!"

"You can't prove that," insisted Ellen. "Besides, if Mr. Hardwell thinks you're spying on him, you could be in real danger. Just promise me you'll stay out of his way."

"I can't make that promise," said Tess stubbornly, "but I'll be careful."

"I guess that'll have to do," said Ellen, as she turned out the light and crawled into bed.

Tess moved to her own bed and sat in the dark. She angrily played her conversation with Ellen over and over in her head.

Even my own sister doubts my story, but I'll show her. I'll keep watching Mr. Hardwell until I get the concrete proof I need.

The next afternoon, Tess and Ellen knocked on the Wrights' door. Miss Wright greeted them wearing her winter coat.

"We're not having lessons inside today, girls," she said. "I thought it would be fun if we watched Tess give her new kite a trial run."

Just then Orville Wright, wearing his overcoat, trooped down the stairs whistling a cheerful tune.

"Ellen and I are going to tag along," said Miss Wright to her brother. "Tess's kite should have an audience for its maiden voyage."

When the group arrived at the cycle shop, Mr. Wright unlocked the side door and let Tess in. As she walked over to the workbench, she remembered Mr. Hardwell's telephone conversation.

I wonder if I should tell Mr. Wright what I over-heard last night? I'd like to tell him, but Ellen says I should keep my nose out of Mr. Hardwell's business. I don't know what to do. Maybe I'd better wait until I've thought about this some more.

Tess picked up her kite and carried it out of the store. Mr. Wright locked the door behind her and they were on their way again.

After walking a few blocks, they reached an open field. Tess looked across the stretch of land. It was the perfect spot to fly a kite. Ellen and Miss Wright stood at the edge of the brown grass while Tess and Mr. Wright hiked to the middle of the field.

Tess held the kite's ball of string and started running. Mr. Wright ran behind Tess, holding the kite up high. When the wind caught the kite, he let it go. The kite sailed toward the billowy clouds, then dipped dangerously close to the ground. Finally a sudden gust seized it and Tess watched her dream take flight.

Ellen and Miss Wright cheered and clapped. Mr. Wright stood back with his arm shielding his eyes from the late afternoon sun and grinned. Tess was flying this kite on her own.

Watching the box kite ascend towards the heavens, Tess whispered with tears in her eyes, "I did it, Papa! I did it for us!"

*   *   *

On Saturday at Owen's Emporium, Tess was carrying a stack of hatboxes to the back of the store when she saw Mr. Hardwell. He was talking to a sales clerk in the leather goods department and pointing to a large black suitcase. He seemed edgy and kept glancing around. He hurriedly reached into his pocket to hand some dollar bills to the clerk. When the salesman left the department to get Mr. Hardwell's change, Tess went over to speak to the photographer.

"Hello, Mr. Hardwell. Are you going on a trip?" she asked.

When the photographer saw Tess, a startled expression crossed his face.

"Well, if you must know," said Mr. Hardwell curtly, "I'm . . . I'm having the store ship this to a friend."

"That's a really nice gift," commented Tess.

She waited for a response, but after an awkward silence, she gave up trying to make conversation.

"Well, I'd better be on my way," she said, glancing down at her hatboxes. "I'll see you later."

That night at the boardinghouse Tess was tired, so she went to bed early. Around midnight, however, she was awakened by Fluffy's cries from the backyard.

Fluffy's finally home and she wants to come in.

Wearily, she slipped on her robe and went down the back stairs. When Tess unlatched the door, Fluffy was waiting on the landing, her tail switching impatiently. She leaned down and picked up the cat.

Tess was halfway to the kitchen when a sudden noise at the back door stopped her in her tracks. She listened a moment. Someone was entering the house! Holding Fluffy tightly, she quickly hid in the broom closet under the stairs. Leaving the door slightly open, Tess strained to see who the intruder was.

"Meow!"

"Be quiet, Fluffy," she whispered into the cat's ear.

Tess held her breath as she watched a man bringing a black suitcase into the house.

Her heart pounded and she squeezed Fluffy tighter. The cat meowed in protest.

"Who's there?" demanded the man. Tess knew that voice. It belonged to Mr. Hardwell.

She heard him move closer to the broom closet.

Tess shrank further into the darkness. Fluffy meowed again. Then jumping from Tess's arms, the cat darted out across Mr. Hardwell's boots.

"Oh, Miss Harriet's stupid cat," he grumbled, kicking Fluffy out of the way.

Fluffy let out a yowl and scurried off to the kitchen. Mr. Hardwell picked up the suitcase and

lugged it upstairs. As soon as Tess heard his bedroom door shut, she tiptoed up the front staircase
and escaped to her room.

*Why did Mr. Hardwell lie about the suitcase and
then sneak it up to his room? What's he going to do
next?*

Tess thought about Mr. Hardwell's odd actions
until she fell asleep.

After school on Monday, Tess and Ellen were listening to Miss Wright read a poem from the book
Oak and Ivy by Paul Laurence Dunbar.

"Paul Laurence Dunbar was one of Orville's
friends at Central High School," she explained.
"Orville helped Mr. Dunbar find a place to print
this little book and he is now a famous poet. He has
written . . ."

"Please excuse the interruption, ladies," said Mr.
Wright, entering the parlor.

"The propellers are ready and I'm off to join
Wilbur in North Carolina. If the weather holds,
Wilbur and I will be able to test the Flyer before
Christmas. And yes, Tess, I promise to give you a
full report."

*Oh no! Mr. Wright is leaving. I want to tell him
about Mr. Hardwell, but I still don't have any evidence
to back up my story.*

Before Tess could decide what to do, Mr. Wright
left the parlor. He took his overcoat from the hall
closet, picked up his satchel, and walked toward the
train station.

All through the rest of Miss Wright's poetry lesson,

Tess's mind wandered. She was upset about Mr. Hardwell, upset with herself for not having told Mr. Wright her suspicions, and there was something else, too. Some thing, some fact she needed to remember.

Later that evening, Tess was reading in her bedroom when she heard the door at the end of the hall open and shut. She ran to the back hallway window just in time to see Mr. Hardwell leaving the boardinghouse.

That's what I was trying to remember! Mr. Hardwell told his partner he was going to the cycle shop as soon as Mr. Wright left for Kitty Hawk.

Tess grabbed her jacket and followed Mr. Hardwell. The others were downstairs trimming the Christmas tree, so she was able to leave the house unnoticed. When she neared the cycle shop, Tess saw Mr. Hardwell turn into the narrow alley and go to the side door. He took a small file from his pocket and expertly picked the lock. Then he opened the door and stepped inside the Wrights' workroom.

I can't see what he's doing in there. I need to get a closer look.

Tess moved quickly to the front door of the cycle shop and peered inside the store. The door separating the two rooms was open and a single candle gave off a faint light. She saw Mr. Hardwell taking sketches of the Flyer's motor off the wall! He carefully folded the pieces of paper and tucked them into the inside pocket of his gray suit coat.

Minutes later, the candle went out in the back room. Tess ran across the street and hid behind some evergreen bushes. She waited until she could no longer hear the clicking sound his boots made on the brick street. Tess sprang from her hiding place and ran through the darkness back to the boardinghouse.

She quietly entered the boardinghouse through the back door. After removing her jacket, she joined the others around the Christmas tree in the parlor.

At bedtime Tess left her door slightly open. She waited until she heard Mr. Hardwell leave his room and go into the lavatory. Quickly Tess ran into Mr. Hardwell's room to look for the motor sketches. She closed the door softly behind her. Through the wall, Tess could hear the bathroom water running. She turned on the bedroom light.

Tess scanned the room looking for Mr. Hardwell's gray suit coat, but the closet and the dresser drawers were empty. Then she noticed a packed suitcase on the bed. As Tess rummaged through the clothes, she found an envelope. The return address was Pittsburgh! She opened the envelope and pulled out a letter.

Suddenly she realized the sound of running water had stopped. Quickly pocketing the letter, she stuffed the envelope back into the suitcase. She turned out the light and dove under the bed just before Mr. Hardwell came into the room.

Tess lay motionless, afraid to make a sound. She saw the light come on and Mr. Hardwell's boots approach the bed. She heard him snap the suitcase shut and set it on the floor. She watched his boots walk out the room and heard the door close as the room went black.

When Tess thought it was safe, she crawled from under the bed and scurried back to her room. She went to the window to read the letter by moonlight.

Hardwell–

> *The Wright brothers are getting too close.*
> *Take the next train and get to Kitty Hawk.*
> *Do whatever it takes to stop them,*
> *even if it means destroying the Wright Flyer!*
> *DO NOT DELAY!!*

J. R. Maddox

SEVEN

ONE STEP BEHIND

A T LAST TESS HAD THE PROOF SHE NEED-
ed! She ran over to Ellen's bed.

"Wake up, wake up!" cried Tess as she shook her sister.

"What is it *now*, Tess?" Ellen propped herself up on one elbow and yawned.

"Mr. Hardwell's gone!" said Tess waving the letter at Ellen. "This explains everything. Read it."

Tess held her tongue while Ellen read the letter. When Ellen finished, Tess saw a look of confusion on her sister's face.

"Don't you understand, Ellen? Mr. Hardwell is already on his way to Kitty Hawk to wreck the Wright Flyer. I knew he and his partner were up to no good. I've got to tell Miss Wright about this so she can warn her brothers."

"You can't do that," said Ellen. "Miss Wright and her father left town for a few days to visit relatives. You'll have to wait until they get back."

"It'll be too late then," said Tess anxiously. "If Miss Wright can't notify her brothers, then I'll have to warn them myself. This letter is the proof I need to put a stop to Mr. Hardwell's plan. There's no other way. I must go to Kitty Hawk!"

"Be reasonable, Tess. You can't go to Kitty Hawk by yourself. It's a long way from here. Besides, if Mr. Hardwell *is* there, it could be dangerous for you. Just wait until morning and talk to Miss Harriet. She'll know what to do."

"Maybe I should contact the police," suggested Tess hesitantly.

"The police won't listen to you," said Ellen impatiently. "That policeman thinks you made up the story about a robbery at the Wrights' home. He told everyone there was no evidence of a break-in and nothing was missing. Seriously Tess, we don't want to cause any trouble here. Miss Harriet might send us back to New York City. So forget you ever found that letter. Just turn off the light and go to sleep!"

Tess got into bed, but she only pretended to sleep.

I don't care what my worrywart sister says. I'm taking Mr. Hardwell's letter to Kitty Hawk. Tonight!

As soon as she heard her sister's even breathing, Tess took the carpetbag from under Ellen's bed. She filled it with a few clothes and the rest of her money. Then she folded Mr. Hardwell's letter and put it next to the coins.

After dressing warmly, she took her bag down to the kitchen. Tess filled a jar with water and packed it in her bag along with some bread and cheese. She gave Fluffy a pat on the head and left for the train station.

It was a cold walk and several times Tess almost turned back. She kept remembering Ellen's warning about the length and dangers of the trip. Tess knew Miss Harriet would have every right to be angry with her as well.

I'm sure I've made the right decision to help my new friends. Somehow, I think Papa and Mama would approve of my actions. I've got to save the Wright Flyer!

Tess pushed open the heavy door of the train station and was grateful for the rush of warm air. A few people were milling around the station, but Tess did not see Mr. Hardwell. She walked over to the ticket counter and rang the bell for service.

After several moments, a sleepy-looking man appeared behind the bars in the booth.

"Yes?" said the clerk in a bored manner.

"I need a ticket to Elizabeth City, North Carolina, please," said Tess politely.

The man leaned forward and studied her for a minute. Then he shrugged his shoulders and replied, "Well, you'll need to go to Norfolk, Virginia, and then change trains to Elizabeth City."

The clerk took Tess's money and handed her a ticket.

"Train's due to pull out in five minutes. The sleeper cars are filled, but there's a passenger car at the back. The conductor will help you aboard."

Tess heard the train's whistle blow and hurried out to the passenger car. After giving her ticket to the conductor, she quickly looked around for Mr.

Hardwell. Relieved he was nowhere to be seen, she sat down by a window. She put her carpetbag under the seat and made herself comfortable. The swaying motion of the car soothed her and eventually Tess dozed off, but her sleep was fitful. Each time the conductor passed through the car, she was awakened by the jingle of his keys.

The next day, Tess spent most of the time gazing out the window at the little towns and farms along the route. The boredom of riding long hours made her feel like she was back on the orphan train. When the train stopped at stations along the way, some passengers got off to buy food. Afraid of running into Mr. Hardwell, however, Tess stayed on board, eating the bread and cheese she'd packed.

As she sipped her water, Tess made plans. She was scared without her older sister, but she tried to keep focused on her mission.

When I get to Norfolk, I must find the train going to Elizabeth City. Once I get there, I'll need to get directions to the docks. Then I'll have to find someone to take me across Albemarle Sound to Kitty Hawk.

When she finished her meager meal, Tess put her jar of water and her remaining piece of cheese back in her bag. Then, glancing around the car, she spotted a newspaper on an empty seat. Tess picked it up and read until she fell asleep.

The next morning Tess woke up to the loud call of the conductor. "Norfolk. Norfolk, Virginia."

Tess got directions from the conductor for her transfer to Elizabeth City. Then she found her next train. She thought she saw Mr. Hardwell climbing onto the train two cars ahead of hers, but she wasn't sure. Quickly hopping aboard she took a seat by herself.

That afternoon, Tess's train pulled into the depot at Elizabeth City. As she stopped to ask the porter for directions to the docks, Tess spotted a small black dog on the tracks. The terrier was straining to unhook his collar which was snagged on a crosstie nail. At the same time, a departing train blew its whistle and started moving toward the struggling animal.

Without stopping to think, Tess dropped her bag and ran to the dog's rescue. Frantically, she worked until she freed his collar. She scooped up the terrier and jumped away from the tracks just in time.

"Buster! Buster!" called a teenaged boy. He ran to Tess and reached out for his frightened little dog.

"Thank you for saving Buster. He ran off after a squirrel and the next thing I knew, you were rescuing him."

"I'm glad he's all right," said Tess. She patted the little dog, and Buster wagged his tail. "I love animals. When I saw he was in trouble, I had to help him."

"I'll always be grateful. Buster means a lot to me," said the boy. "By the way, my name is Mac McDonnell."

"Nice to meet you. I'm Tess Raney. I was about to ask for directions to the docks. Do you know how to get there?"

"Sure," replied Mac. "I work at the docks with my grandpa. I'd take you there now, but I have to run some errands for him."

Mac pointed to some tall masts that were visible above the buildings.

"See the tops of those sailboats? Walk toward them and you'll be there in no time."

Tess thanked Mac, retrieved her bag, and headed toward the waterfront. As she walked along the boardwalk, afternoon clouds began to cover the sun and blowing sea spray left the taste of salt on her lips.

Suddenly Tess was shoved from behind! Her bag fell to the ground as she was pushed into a dark, windowless shed. She heard the door slam and the bolt slide into place.

"Be quiet in there or else!"

Mr. Hardwell!

"You spied on me in Dayton, but I can't believe you followed me all the way here!" Mr. Hardwell said. "This will put an end to your sleuthing once and for all."

Tess heard him laugh as he walked away, leaving her alone in the dark. She slumped into a heap and began to cry.

No one knows where I am. I should have listened to Ellen. Now I'll never be able to save the Flyer.

Tess cried until her eyes were red and swollen. Then digging deep inside herself, she found courage.

Crying will get me nowhere. Papa always said, "God helps those who help themselves."

Tess crawled through the dark until she found the door. She began beating her fists against the boards.

"Help! Help!" cried Tess. "I'm locked in here!"

Tess yelled and yelled until her throat ached, but

no one came. She sat back down and took deep breaths, trying to calm her rising panic.

Just then, she heard something. Tess jumped to her feet and listened at the crack in the door. She could hear a dog barking outside. Tess began to pound with all her might.

"What's in there, Buster? Have you cornered another squirrel?"

Tess's heart skipped a beat and she hollered, "Mac, is that you? It's Tess. I'm locked in here!"

Tess heard the bolt slide back and watched Mac throw open the shed door. She stumbled out into the light and sat down, breathing in gulps of fresh air as her swollen eyes adjusted to the light. Buster ran up and licked the tears of relief that covered her face.

Mac knelt down. "Tess, what happened? Are you all right?"

Suddenly Tess remembered the letter and began searching wildly for her carpetbag.

Mac found the carpetbag behind the shed door and held it up.

"Is this what you're looking for?"

"That's it!" cried Tess.

She grabbed the bag and anxiously looked inside. The letter of proof and her money were still there!

"Is anything missing?" asked Mac.

"No," Tess replied. "I was afraid the man who locked me in the shed had robbed me."

"Why did he lock you up if he didn't want your money?" questioned Mac. "It doesn't make any sense."

"No it doesn't," said Tess. She didn't want to talk

about Mr. Hardwell. It was a long story and she had no time to waste.

"Well, whatever the reason, he's probably miles from here by now. At least you're safe," said Mac. "Now, where are you headed?"

"I must get to Kitty Hawk right away," said Tess.

"Maybe I can help," said Mac. "I'm first mate on my grandpa's sailboat. He has to deliver some supplies to the Outer Banks, so he might be willing to take you along tonight. Let's ask him if you can hitch a ride with us."

Tess followed Mac to a small sailboat sitting low in the water. The paint was peeling off its wooden deck, but otherwise it appeared seaworthy. An old man with a weather-beaten face looked up from loading supplies onto the deck.

"Grandpa, I want you to meet my new friend, Tess Raney," called Mac. "Tess, this is my grandfather, Captain Zeb."

"Pleased to meet you," responded the old salt.

"Tess needs a ride to Kitty Hawk right now," said Mac. "Since we're making a supply run tonight anyway, I thought we might take her along."

"It's at least a twelve-hour trip, a long haul for a young lady. Why do you need to go there?" asked the captain.

"I have some vital information to deliver to the Wright brothers at their camp," explained Tess. "Mr. Orville Wright is a friend of mine."

"Well, if the trip is that important to you," said Captain Zeb, "then climb aboard."

Holding her carpetbag, Tess gingerly stepped onto the deck and sat down on a wooden bench. Mac whistled for Buster and they jumped on.

Tess willed the small boat to go faster, but it just drifted along at an even pace. Finally a brisk wind caught the sails and drew the sloop toward Albemarle Sound. By the time they entered the sound, it was getting dark.

Tess felt a weariness in her bones and her eyelids began to droop. She stretched out on the bench. Buster came over and settled next to her. The gentle lapping of the waves soon lulled Tess into a deep sleep.

Suddenly Tess woke up with cold rain pricking her face like tiny needles. Waves splashed against the boat, sending icy sprays of water into the air. The sailboat began to rock unsteadily in the choppy sea.

Tess sat up and called in a trembling voice, "What's happening, Mac?"

"We've run into a little bad weather," he yelled back. "Just hang on."

Mac threw Tess a life jacket and she struggled into it. Then he went over to man the ropes.

"It's all right, Tess," called Captain Zeb from the wheel. "Sometimes we get these squalls, but they never last long."

Tess pulled her scarf around her neck and braced herself against the bench. She heard Buster whimpering so she called him to come to her. Picking up the frightened terrier, Tess held him in her lap to ride out the storm.

EIGHT

First Flight!

THE NEXT MORNING TESS SAW LARGE SAND dunes outlined against the gray backdrop of dawn. Captain Zeb was skillfully guiding the boat toward the pier while Mac handled the ropes. She stood up, stretched her cramped muscles, and gazed across the calm ocean waters.

"Is that Kitty Hawk?" asked Tess.

"Yes," answered Mac. "We're almost there."

When the sailboat drew near the dock, Mac jumped off and tied the line to a piling. Tess picked up her carpetbag and stepped onto the pier.

"Thank you both for getting me here safely. Now I must get to the Wrights' camp immediately."

Mac pointed to an unpainted house with a wide verandah a quarter of a mile away.

"Go see Mrs. Tate over at the post office," said Mac. "She'll give you directions."

Tess stooped down and spoke to the little black dog.

"Goodbye, Buster. Be a good dog and stay off the train tracks!"

Buster wagged his tail and started to follow her. Mac

called the terrier back and picked him up. Tess took a few steps, waved once, then walked hurriedly away.

When Tess arrived at the house she saw a sign that read, *Kitty Hawk, North Carolina Post Office*. She found a dark-haired woman sorting mail behind the counter.

"Are you Mrs. Tate?" asked Tess.

"Why, yes I am, child," she answered. "Do you need some help?

"Yes, please. I'm Tess Raney and I have an important message for Mr. Orville Wright. Could you tell me how to get to the Wrights' camp?"

"You know, it's odd," said Mrs. Tate, setting down the letters. "You're the second person to come here this morning asking directions to the Wrights' place. There was a real nice gent who came by earlier. Said he was a photographer from Dayton."

"How long ago was that, Mrs. Tate?" asked Tess, her face clouded with concern.

"Less than an hour, I suppose," she answered. "He seemed real anxious to get to the camp."

"I need to go too," Tess quickly reminded the talkative postmistress.

"Oh, of course. The camp's about four miles south of here. Just follow the path along the bay and you'll see the tower of the Kill Devil Hills Lifesaving Station. Some of the lifesavers go to help the brothers when they test their Flyer. If the Wrights are conducting their experiments today, you'll see a signal flag flying over the two large buildings near some high sand dunes called Kill Devil Hills. That's the camp."

"Could I leave my carpetbag here?" asked Tess.

"It's too heavy for me to carry that distance."

"Of course," said Mrs. Tate. "I'll keep it right behind the counter."

Before Tess handed Mrs. Tate the bag, she opened it and took out the letter of proof. She folded it carefully and slid it into her skirt pocket.

Tess left the post office and started running down a path flanked on either side with sparse clumps of grass and low scrub trees. She was tired and her clothes were still damp from the boat ride, but she forced herself onward in her race against time. Tess kept her eyes on the road, watching for slippery puddles of frozen rainwater.

Startled by a gull's screech, Tess looked up. At that moment, she slipped on a patch of ice and her feet went out from under her. She cried out as a pain shot through her right ankle. After a moment, Tess cautiously stood up and tried a few steps. Her ankle throbbed, so she sat back down. Removing her scarf, she wound it around her ankle for support. Then slowly she got up and started off again.

Now I've got to make myself hurry even more. As Miss Carsdale always said to Ellen and me, "Keep moving, girls!"

As Tess climbed over the small crest of a sand dune, the camp buildings came into view. Three men in uniform were coming out of a wooden building, carrying long pieces of track. Through the wide door Tess could see the Flyer!

Just then, the door of the smaller building opened and Orville Wright stepped out.

Tess started limping down the sand dunes waving her arms to attract his attention.

"Mr. Wright!" cried Tess. "Mr. Wright!"

At the sound of her voice, he turned. A look of surprise crossed his face.

"Tess! What in the world are you doing here?" asked Mr. Wright.

"I've come to warn you about Mr. Hardwell!" cried Tess. "He's trying to sabotage your Flyer!"

"Oh, Tess," replied Mr. Wright. "Mr. Hardwell's here to take pictures of the Flyer."

"He's lying to you. I saw him steal your motor sketches from the cycle shop!" cried Tess, words tumbling out of her mouth. "I overheard Mr. Hardwell talking to his partner on the telephone. Mr. Hardwell told him he had stolen notebooks from your father's study and mailed them to Pittsburgh."

"I'm sorry, Tess, but I'm having trouble believing all of this."

Tears of frustration welled up in her eyes. Tess knew she had to save the Flyer. Reaching into her skirt pocket, she drew out the letter and gave it to Mr. Wright.

"Read this," pleaded Tess. "I found it in Mr. Hardwell's suitcase. It proves that Mr. Hardwell is planning to sabotage your flying machine."

Tess stood anxiously while Mr. Wright read the letter.

"Are you certain Mr. Hardwell's partner wrote this?" asked Mr. Wright.

"Yes, I'm sure," answered Tess. "I heard Mr. Hardwell call him J. R. on the telephone and the letter is signed J. R. Maddox."

She watched as Mr. Wright's expression changed from one of doubt to one of anger.

"We have no time to waste, Tess! All the men are outside laying the movable track and I just gave Mr. Hardwell permission to take pictures of the Flyer in the hangar. Let's go!"

When they got to the hangar, a man in a gray suit coat was poised over the Flyer's motor, a heavy wrench in his hand.

"Stop!" commanded Mr. Wright. "What are you doing to our machine?"

Whirling around in surprise, Mr. Hardwell dropped the wrench to the floor.

"Oh, Mr. Wright, you startled me," he replied, "I was just . . ."

Suddenly Mr. Hardwell saw Tess standing behind Mr. Wright in the hangar's doorway. Without another word, he bolted from the hangar and ran toward the road.

"Stop that man!" yelled Mr. Wright to the lifesavers close by.

One of the men sprinted after Mr. Hardwell and grabbed his leg. While he wrestled him to the ground, another man ran up with a piece of rope and tied the photographer's hands together. The two lifesavers roughly pulled Mr. Hardwell to his feet and held him firmly between them.

The rest of the camp heard Mr. Wright's shouts and everyone ran to see what was happening. When Tess and Mr. Wright joined the group, she noticed one man was wearing a business suit with a high collar, just like Mr. Wright always wore.

That must be Mr. Wright's older brother, Wilbur.

"What's going on here?" asked Wilbur Wright. "And why on earth is Mr. Hardwell tied up?"

"Mr. Wright and I caught him trying to destroy the Flyer," Tess blurted out.

"She's telling the truth," confirmed Orville Wright. "We found him by the motor holding a wrench."

"There's more," said Tess earnestly. "Mr. Hardwell is a thief! He's working with a partner and a team in Pittsburgh. They've been stealing your ideas so they can be the first ones to fly. Check his inside coat pocket. You'll find your motor sketches there."

Mr. Hardwell struggled to get free, but the two lifesavers tightened their grip on his arms. One of the men grabbed Mr. Hardwell's coat pocket and pulled out the stack of sketches.

"I've heard and seen more than enough, Hardwell," said Orville Wright, shaking his head in disgust. "Take this man to the police."

"You rotten little snoop!" Mr. Hardwell snarled at Tess. "Why couldn't you just mind your own business?"

The burly lifesavers force-marched the guilty man away.

"Well done, Tess," said Orville Wright. "Thanks to you, we can continue our flying experiments today right on schedule."

"You're a brave young woman!" agreed Wilbur Wright. "Orville has told me how much you like flying, but your determination to help us is nothing short of amazing. Come inside and warm up by the stove. Then you can watch us test the Flyer."

"Could I really?" asked Tess.

"Of course," said Wilbur Wright. A friendly smile replaced his serious expression. "You, of all people, should see how our flying machine works."

Tess followed the Wright brothers into the building that served as their living quarters. She sat by the wood-burning stove and warmed her cold, chapped hands. While Wilbur Wright made tea, his brother checked Tess's ankle and re-wrapped it tightly.

"It's not broken," he said, "I think it's just twisted. Prop it up on this bucket while you rest."

After a soothing cup of hot tea and a biscuit, Tess's ankle felt better. She was ready to watch the flying experiments. She pulled on her jacket and went outside.

As the wind and sand swirled, Tess watched the life-savers roll the 650-pound Wright Flyer out of the hangar onto the 60-foot monorail that stretched across level ground. They pushed the Flyer along the moveable track, occasionally stopping to let men go to the back and move one of the 15-foot track pieces to the front. When the Flyer was in position, Orville placed a camera on a tripod near the track's base. Wilbur instructed one of the lifesavers to take a photograph at liftoff.

Then each Wright brother grabbed a propeller and spun it. The motor jumped to life! While the engine warmed up, Wilbur and Orville walked a little way down the beach and stood by themselves talking for a while.

Tess saw the brothers shaking hands. It was as though they were saying goodbye to each other forever. At that moment, Tess realized just how dangerous these flying experiments were.

Tess watched closely as Orville Wright climbed into the Flyer. He stretched out on his stomach and positioned himself to test the hip cradle. When Mr. Wright shifted his hips from side to side, the cradle pulled on cables which warped the wing tips.

He hooked his shoes into a small rack near the edge of the wing. Next, he released the holding wire and the flying machine moved down the track into the face of a 27-mile-per-hour wind. Holding a wing to keep the machine on track, Wilbur ran alongside it until the Flyer lifted off the level ground under its own power. The flying machine was in the air!

Tess and the lifesavers cheered wildly as the flying machine rose. It traveled about 120 feet, then dove toward the ground. The flight was over. It had lasted only twelve seconds, but Tess was sure she had witnessed something special. She knew that December 17, 1903, was a date that would be burned in her memory forever. Tess felt her spirits soar.

Three other flights were made that day with the brothers taking turns at the controls. At noontime, Tess watched Wilbur Wright make the last and longest flight of the day. She marveled as the twirling propellers, muslin-covered wings, and noisy motor lifted the flying machine into the air. Suddenly, the Flyer came down and plowed into the sand, smashing the front rudder frame. Tess held her breath until Wilbur signaled that he was all right.

"That flight went 852 feet in 59 seconds! Definitely, the longest flight today!" announced one of the life-savers. The men shouted their congratulations to the brothers, lending a touch of celebration to the cold, bleak day.

After the men hauled the Flyer back near the hanger, a sudden gust of wind caught the wings and tipped it over. Both Wright brothers and their helpers battled the wind trying to steady the Flyer. Only one man, however, was able to hold onto the machine. The Flyer flipped crazily across the sand with the poor man trapped inside. When the shaken man rolled safely out onto the sand, a loud hurrah rose from the crowd.

Tess watched the lifesavers take the damaged machine back into the hangar. They slapped each other heartily on the back and said their goodbyes. There would be no more flights in 1903. The Wright brothers had accomplished their goal and now they could go home for Christmas.

"Let's go to Kitty Hawk," suggested Wilbur, fishing a bill out of his pocket. "We'll use Father's dollar to telegraph our good news."

"Good idea," agreed Orville. "We can send a telegram to Miss Harriet, too. Tess, do you think your ankle will hold up for the hike?"

"Yes, my ankle feels fine now," Tess answered.

They all started down the sandy path. Tess tried to keep up with the long strides of the Wrights, but soon lagged behind. She began to think about facing Miss Harriet.

How am I going to make Miss Harriet understand that I had to come here?

Tess was weary. She walked with her head down, concentrating on placing one foot in front of the other. Just when she thought she couldn't take another step, Orville Wright called back to her, "Tess, look who's here!"

Tess looked up. Miss Harriet and Ellen were on the post office porch! She anxiously studied their faces, trying to read their mood.

"Tess!" cried Miss Harriet clamoring down the steps. "My brave girl! We just arrived when one of the lifesaving men came by the post office. He told us what happened at the Wrights' camp this morning. We're all so proud of you!"

Miss Harriet and Ellen ran toward Tess, arms wide open to welcome her. Tess felt herself encircled in a warm embrace.

"My dear child," cried Miss Harriet, tears of joy streaming down her cheeks. "We've come to take you home!"

Tess smiled at the thought and her heart nearly burst with happiness as she pictured it.

Home.

Suddenly Tess's smile widened into a huge grin. A white ball of fur jumped out of Miss Harriet's basket and was scampering towards her. She scooped up Fluffy and hugged her, too.

"Yes," said Tess, love shining in her eyes as she gazed at her family, "let's go home."

Historical Postscript

Tess and Ellen Raney are fictional characters. They weren't really neighbors of the Wrights. Their adoption by Miss Harriet, however, was much like that of the orphan children who rode the Orphan Trains from 1854 to 1929.

Wilbur and Orville Wright were real people. They grew up in a loving home on Hawthorn Street in Dayton, Ohio. Milton and Susan Wright encouraged their children's curiosity. The Wright brothers inherited their mother's mechanical ability. Susan died in 1889 and never saw her sons' first flight. Katharine was the younger sister of Wilbur and Orville. She devoted her life to helping them achieve their dreams.

A toy helicopter sparked the Wright brothers' first interest in flying. Wilbur and Orville then progressed to building kites, gliders, and finally the Wright Flyer. The Wright brothers enjoyed working as a team. Together they uncovered the secrets of aviation. They designed a lightweight motor using hand-drawn sketches. They also developed wing-warping, a technique to control the direction of the flying machine by flexing the wings. Using this method, the Wright brothers were able to *control and sustain* their Flyer in the air.

The Wright brothers chose Kitty Hawk, North Carolina, to test the Flyer. They needed constant winds for flying and soft sands for landing. Flying their machine into the wind helped the engine provide the lift they needed for takeoff. Just as Tess's kite was pulled into the wind by its strings, so the Wright Flyer was pulled into the wind by its propellers.

Tess followed the route the Wright brothers took to reach Kitty Hawk. The Kill Devil Hills camp described in the story actually existed. Wilbur and Orville lived in one wooden building. The Flyer was housed in the other.

The Wright brothers worked tirelessly conducting flight experiments at their camp. Competition to build the first controllable, motor-powered flying machine was keen. Although Mr. Hardwell and J. R. Maddox were not real competitors, there were people competing with the Wrights. When Wilbur and Orville discovered *how to control flight*, they moved ahead of their competition.

Men from the lifesaving stations engaged in sea rescues along the Outer Banks. The lifesavers helped Wilbur and Orville lay the moveable track. Then they rolled the Flyer into a launching position. Captain Jesse E. Ward was the station keeper at Kill Devil Hills Lifesaving Station in 1903. His grandson drew the illustrations for this book!

On December 17, 1903, Orville, aged thirty-two, took the controls of the Flyer. He made the first successful controlled, motor-powered flight from level ground. It lasted only twelve seconds. Three other successful flights were completed by noon. The last and longest was by Wilbur Wright, aged thirty-six. It flew 852 feet in 59 seconds. After four flights, a sudden gust of wind turned the Flyer over. The damage to the Flyer ended the experiments for 1903.

That afternoon the Wright brothers walked four miles to Kitty Hawk. They sent a telegram home announcing their news—news that would lift the barrier between earth and sky, changing the course of history forever.

WRIGHT BROTHERS NATIONAL MEMORIAL
OUTER BANKS, NORTH CAROLINA

NORTH ELEVATION OF MONUMENT

You can visit the actual site on the Outer Banks of North Carolina where the Wright brothers conducted their flight experiments. At the Visitor Center you can see a full-size model reproduction of the 1903 Wright Flyer. A large pavilion houses interactive exhibits and displays about the past, present, and future of aviation. Outside, trails lead to replicas of the camp buildings that served as Wilbur and Orville's residence and work-shop. Information about the flights is written on stone markers placed at the spots where the Flyer landed. Also on display are segments of moveable track.

At Kill Devil Hill stands the Wright Monument, a 60-foot-tall pylon. Pylons—tall towers—were commonly used as landmarks to guide pilots during early air competitions and cross-country flights. In the 1930s a nationwide contest was held to come up with a fitting tribute to the two pioneering brothers. The winning design, selected from among 36 entries, stands atop 90-foot-tall Kill Devil Hill. The towering monument is a granite pylon with gigantic wings worked into the sides. The monument's stainless steel doors are decorated with eight panels depicting man's early attempts at mechanical flight, from the Greek legend of Icarus to early kites and balloons. Inside are busts of Orville, Wilbur, and a model of the Wright Flyer. Work began on the winning design in December 1931. The monument was dedicated a year later on a stormy November 19, 1932. The beacon, first lit in 1937, was extinguished during World War II. The monument was then rededicated in May 1998, its beacon relit for the first time in over fifty years.

Proceeds from the sale of this book help First Flight Centennial® Foundation make improvements to the Wright Brothers National Memorial so that many generations of children may be inspired to let their dreams take flight.